E FIN
Fine, Edith Hope.
Armando and the blue tarp
school / by Edith Hope Fine
and Judith Pinkerton
Josephson ; illustrated by

CALIFORNIA INSTITUTE OF
TECHNOLOGY LIBRARY
PASADENA, CALIFORNIA
INSTITUTE ARCHIVES

Armando and the Blue Tarp School

by **Edith Hope Fine** and **Judith Pinkerton Josephson**

illustrated by **Hernán Sosa**

FOUNTAINDALE PUBLIC LIBRARY DISTRICT
300 West Briarcliff Road
Bolingbrook, IL 60440-2894
(630) 759-2102

BIENVENIDOS

WELCOME

Lee & Low Books Inc. *New York*

Acknowledgments

For their insight and suggestions, we send warm thanks to Ira Boroditsch, Vince Compagnone, Hilary Crain, Dora Ficklin, Jill Hansen, Pat Hatfield, Melissa Irick, Kirsten Josephson, Catherine Koemptgen, David Lynch, Sara Morgan, Joany Mosher, Alicia Muñoz, Anne Otterson, Sarai Padron, Esmeralda Rodriguez, Izamar Sanchez, Rosalinda Quintanar-Sarellana, Hernán Sosa, Olga Stebbins, the intuitive members of our critique group, and our editor, Louise May. —*E.H.F.* and *J.P.J.*

A portion of the proceeds from this book will be donated to Responsibility, Inc. (responsibilityonline.org), the foundation that supports David Lynch's work with the children of Mexico.

Text copyright © 2007 by Edith Hope Fine and Judith Pinkerton Josephson
Illustrations copyright © 2007 by Hernán Sosa
All rights reserved. No part of this book may be reproduced, transmitted, or stored in an information retrieval system in any form or by any means, electronic, mechanical, photocopying, recording, or otherwise, without written permission from the publisher.
LEE & LOW BOOKS Inc., 95 Madison Avenue, New York, NY 10016
leeandlow.com
Manufactured in China
Book design by Christy Hale
Book production by The Kids at Our House
The text is set in Zapf Humanist
The illustrations are rendered in masking fluid, watercolor, and ink
10 9 8 7 6 5 4 3 2 1
First Edition
Library of Congress Cataloging-in-Publication Data
Fine, Edith Hope.
Armando and the blue tarp school / by Edith Hope Fine and Judith Pinkerton Josephson ; illustrated by Hernán Sosa. — 1st ed.
p. cm.
Summary: Armando and his father are trash-pickers in Tijuana, Mexico, but when Señor David brings his "school"—a blue tarp set down near the garbage dump—to their neighborhood, Armando's father decides that he must attend classes and learn. Based on a true story.
ISBN-13: 978-1-58430-278-0
[1. Education—Fiction. 2. Poverty—Fiction. 3. Mexico—Fiction.]
I. Josephson, Judith Pinkerton. II. Sosa, Hernán, ill. III. Title.
PZ7.F495674Arm 2007
[E]—dc22   2006036560

For the amazing David Lynch and the many supporters of
Responsibility, Inc. —*E.H.F.* and *J.P.J.*

To my wife Robyn, without whom there is no color —*H.S.*

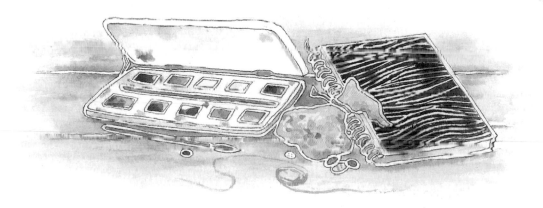

All day Armando and Papá had worked at the dump, picking through trash. Now they trudged down the rocky hillside. Afternoon sunlight shone on broken glass, rickety fences, and tumbledown houses in their *colonia*, their neighborhood.

Buh-beep! Buh-beep! A truck horn blared from below.

Armando pointed. "*¡Mira!* Look, Papá! It's Señor David, from last summer!"

Papá was silent for a moment. Then he said, "You can go. Just this once."

Armando hurried down the gravelly path to tell his friend Isabella the news. Off they ran—down the dirt road, across the wobbly plank, and past the big rock.

"Señor David! You're back!" said Armando.

"My friends, *mis amigos*. I've missed you!"
said Señor David, spreading a big tarp on the ground.

"Your school," Armando said. "I remember."

The first time Señor David called his blue tarp a school,
Armando hadn't understood. He thought schools had walls,
floors, and roofs. But Señor David said a school could be
anywhere—even on a tarp in a *colonia*.

"Ready to learn more?" asked Señor David.

"*¡Sí!*" the children shouted. "Yes!"

Nearby, scrawny chickens pecked at the dirt.

"Hen," said Señor David. He flapped his arms. *"Brawk-brawk-brawk."*

"La gallina . . . hen," said the children. They flapped their arms too. *"Brawk-brawk-brawk."*

On his chalkboard Señor David wrote the letters of the alphabet. The children called out letters in Spanish and English, then practiced words they had learned last year: house—*la casa;* boy—*el muchacho;* girl—*la muchacha.*

"Very good! *¡Muy bien!"* said Señor David. "We'll work hard this summer, but we'll have fun too."

Armando couldn't wait.

That night Armando ate slowly. At last he asked if he could go to school on Señor David's blue tarp.

Papá frowned. "Do not fill your head with dreams of school."

"I went last year," said Armando.

"You are older now," said Papá. "I wish things could be different. But we are *pepenadores*, trash pickers. You must do the work of our family."

Mamá added, "Your sisters are small. I need to stay here with them. The money you and Papá earn helps us live."

Tears stung Armando's eyes. More than anything, he wanted to learn, but he knew Papá and Mamá were right.

Later Armando sat on his thin mattress. With a stubby pencil, he sketched a picture of Señor David's truck.

As Papá and Armando neared the dump the next morning, the foul smell grew stronger and stronger. Rumbling trash trucks backed up. *Eep! Eep! Eep!* Out tumbled heaps of garbage. Workers rushed forward to tear at boxes and rip open plastic bags. Flocks of squawking seagulls circled and dove, fighting over bits of rotting food.

Armando searched for bottles and cans, clothes and toys. Some to sell, some to use. In one tattered bag he found shiny buttons and silvery thread. From another he pulled a smudged notebook and a dented tin of paints. These he kept.

Armando mopped his sweaty face and swatted at buzzing flies. *What was Señor David teaching now?* he wondered.

By the time Armando and Papá headed for home, the sun had dipped low, painting the sky red. Hearing the gate squeak, Isabella raced over to share what she had learned at school. Words covered her paper.

"*La rana* is frog," she said. "We hopped with Señor David. We said *icruá-cruá!* and *ribbit-ribbit!*"

Armando's shoulders drooped. "I wish I could go with you."

"I know," said Isabella. "But I'll bring you new words. I promise."

After Isabella left, Armando copied her words into his notebook. Then he made a picture for each one. Before he went to sleep, he put his notebook and paints with the other treasures on the ledge above his bed.

Every day Armando worked at the dump. And every day he longed
to be sitting on the blue tarp.

One evening Papá said, "People are talking about Señor David's school."
Armando's stomach flip-flopped.

"We have always been *pepenadores*," Papá went on. "But learning is
important. It could help you find different work when you grow up.
Maybe in the city. So Mamá and I decided. You may leave the
dump early—for school."

"But . . . the money . . . ," said Armando.

"Somehow we will manage."

"*Gracias*, Papá. Thank you." Armando hurried outside
to tell Isabella. They whooped with joy.

From then on Armando worked mornings with Papá. Each afternoon Armando and Isabella walked down the dirt road, across the wobbly plank, and past the big rock to Señor David's school.

Sometimes the lessons were easy. Sometimes they were hard. But soon the children could write sentences and do numbers. They sang songs, played games, and drew pictures.

Below a drawing of red flowers, Armando wrote: *Las rosas huelen bien.* Roses smell nice.

By a girl jumping rope, he wrote: *Isabella salta.* Isabella jumps.

One day a cow lumbered by.

"*Hola, vaca,*" said Armando. "*Muuu-muuu.*"

"Hello, cow," said Señor David. "Mooo-mooo. Cows give milk—*la leche.*"

"Cows give milk," echoed the children.

Another day Armando sketched a fat pig snuffling through garbage.

"Great pig! *¡Tremendo cerdo!*" said Señor David.

Then Armando showed him a painting he had made of a tall man with brown hair and a mustache. On it he had written: *Mi amigo.* My friend.

"Is that me?" asked Señor David.

"*Sí,*" said Armando.

"*Gracias, mi amigo,*" said Señor David. He shook Armando's hand.

Week after week Armando wrote, drew, and painted. Soon words, sentences, and bright pictures filled his notebook.

One night the smell of smoke jolted Armando awake. Winds howled. Wood crackled.

"¡Fuego! ¡Fuego!" people shouted. "Fire! Fire!"

Mamá and Papá gathered the children and ran from the house.

Flames roared through the *colonia*. Papá rushed to help. Men slapped at the fire with wet blankets. They threw buckets of water.

Safe on the hillside, Mamá hugged the children close. Heart thudding, Armando watched as a wall of greedy flames swallowed up his house.

At dawn hot ashes smoldered. Many houses had burned. Armando stared at the patch of ground where his family's home had stood. Nothing was left.

Señor David put his hand on Armando's shoulder. "Your words and drawings?"

"*Todo está perdido,*" said Armando in a small, sad voice. "All gone."

"I'm sorry. *Lo siento,*" said Señor David.

Two days later the scent of smoke still hung in the air. Señor David and the children gathered on his blue tarp.

"What a hard time for you, *mis amigos*," he said. "No lessons today. Let's just draw."

Armando colored orange and red flames, black smoke, and frightened faces.

As the children worked, a car drove up.

"Please welcome our visitors," Señor David said. "They're writing a story about the fire and our school for the city newspaper."

The photographer snapped pictures. The reporter scribbled notes. When she spotted Armando's drawing, she asked to borrow it. Armando wondered why. He glanced at Señor David.

"Go ahead, Armando," he said. "It's okay."

The next day Señor David held up a newspaper. "Look! *¡Mira!*" he said. Armando's eyes grew wide. On the front page was his drawing of the fiery night. His picture—for everyone to see! The children cheered. Armando grinned. Señor David gave him a copy of the paper to show Mamá and Papá.

Later that week came another surprise. When a kind woman in the city saw Armando's painting and read the story, she sent money to build a school.

"Where?" asked Armando.

"Right where our blue tarp school has been," said Señor David.

Armando closed his eyes, imagining how the school would look.

Over the next weeks Señor David and Papá built a new house for Armando's family from fence boards, chicken wire, and old garage doors. They helped other families rebuild too.

Whenever people could, they worked on the school. They mixed cement and smoothed out a floor. They sawed wood and pounded nails to build four walls and a sturdy roof. Light poured in where the windows would go.

At last the school was finished. The children crowded inside, chattering and pointing. They darted from benches to tables to books with colorful pictures.

Isabella ran her fingers over the braided blue rug. "It's like our blue tarp!" she said.

Then Armando spotted a wooden easel spattered with paint.

"Your *papá* brought that," said Señor David.

Armando's eyes sparkled. Papá wanted him here, learning and painting. Ever since the first *buh-beep!* of Señor David's truck horn, Armando had longed for such a place. A place to learn. A place to grow. A place for friends.

Armando flung his arms wide. Words tumbled out. "I am happy from here to the sky!"

David Lynch

1980: Teaching children in the *colonia* became David Lynch's lifework.

David Lynch

1983: Students at work with their teacher.

Vince Compagnone

Youngsters head home with their paintings.

Authors' Note

Although this story is fiction, it is based in fact. Señor David is David Lynch, a former special education teacher from New York. He first went to Mexico over the summer of 1980 to teach children living in a *colonia* of the Tijuana city dump. He returned for two more summers, working with youngsters who lived in the shadow of mounds of trash. Convinced that education held the key to these children's futures, Lynch made a decision. He would stay. "There was a magnetic attraction to the people, and that brought me back," Lynch says.

Armando is a composite of children we met at the *colonia*. Like them, he works alongside his father in the dump. He sees beauty in the simplest of things, even though his surroundings are bleak. Neighborhoods like his surround trash dumps in big cities around the world.

Vince Compagnone

Children walking through the *colonia* at the trash dump.

David Lynch's first school was a blue tarp spread on a patch of bare ground. "The children's eagerness to learn amazed me," Lynch notes. "Their attention never wavered, despite a constant parade of pigs, dogs, ducks, and chickens passing through their outdoor classroom." Over time Lynch created a school curriculum that included kindergarten, Mexican culture, and English as a second language.

Like their parents, few of Lynch's students had ever traveled beyond the *colonia*. Lynch talked with the children about school and careers, exposing their young minds to the larger world. In the early days, he took small groups on field trips across the border to San Diego. On several memorable trips to New York City, the children marveled at the tall buildings. With wonder, they touched the cold, hard ice of a skating rink.

We first met David Lynch while freelancing for the *Los Angeles Times* in 1985. One cold December day we visited the Tijuana dump with photographer Vince Compagnone. That day Lynch pulled out jars of paint. Painting was new to most of the youngsters. They relished the texture and scent of the paint, filling their papers with bright colors. We couldn't help but be touched by their eager, open faces.

After our article appeared, our editor at the newspaper called with the news that an anonymous reader had donated money to build a school. For the residents of the *colonia*, having a school of their own had been a dream. At last they had the funds to buy construction materials. They did the work themselves.

Six months later, when the building was completed, we returned with the photographer to do a follow-up story. The whole *colonia* celebrated, and we witnessed the children's jubilation over the opening of their new school.

1986: David Lynch teaching in the new school building.

Excited children on their first day of class.

School founder David Lynch in 2006.

"I am still here, but my hair is gone," jokes David Lynch about his twenty-seven years of teaching at the Tijuana city dump. Responsibility, Inc., a nonprofit organization, now supports Lynch's efforts. Corporations and businesses have donated goods and funds. Lynch has also set up a program linking American high school and college students with needy children. A theater group staged a musical production that highlighted Lynch's work. His story has also attracted the attention of the media and the support of performers, actors, and celebrities, including actress Susan Sarandon and journalist/commentator Bill O'Reilly.

Felipe Quiroz Gonzalez with his students.

Many of Lynch's former students have met with success. One is Felipe Quiroz Gonzalez, a student at the original blue tarp school. Today Quiroz Gonzalez teaches preschoolers and kindergarteners, and is assistant director at the school, now called Escuela David Lynch. "He is a natural teacher," Lynch says of Quiroz Gonzalez.

In November 2006, at UNICEF House at the United Nations in New York City, Lynch was honored with the World of Children Humanitarian Award, which recognizes ordinary people worldwide who do extraordinary work on behalf of children. Because of Lynch, children living near the Tijuana dump envision futures unimaginable before his arrival. They know that learning can change their lives. They dream of careers as lawyers, computer technicians, talk show hosts, teachers, artists, doctors, and more. As Lynch tells them, "The decisions are yours. They're your responsibility."

Through the vision and persistence of David Lynch, thousands of young children and their families have been touched by hope.

Edith Hope Fine and *Judith Pinkerton Josephson*
2007

2006: Preschoolers gather with their hero.

Glossary and Pronunciation Guide

bien (be-EN): nice, good
bienvenidos (be-EN-veh-NEE-dohs): welcome
la casa (la CAH-sah): house
el cerdo (el SER-doh): pig
la colonia (la co-LOW-nee-ah): neighborhood
cruá-cruá (crew-AH-crew-AH): the sound a frog makes
en (ehn): in
está (ess-TAH): is
el fuego (el FWEH-go): fire
la gallina (la gah-YEE-nah): hen

gracias (GRAH-see-ahs): thank you
hola (OH-lah): hello
huelen (WEH-lehn): smell
la leche (la LEH-cheh): milk
lo siento (loh see-EHN-toh): I am (I'm) sorry
la luna (la LOO-nah): moon
mamá (mah-MAH): mother, mom
mi amigo (me ah-MEE-goh): my friend (male)
mira (ME-rah): watch, look
mis amigos (mees ah-MEE-gohs): my friends
la muchacha (la moo-CHA-chah): girl
el muchacho (el moo-CHA-choh): boy
muuu-muuu (moo-moo): the sound a cow makes
muy (MOO-ee): very
papá (pah-PAH): father, dad
los pepenadores (lohs peh-pen-ah-DOH-rehs): trash pickers
perdido (pair-DEE-doh): lost, gone
la rana (la RAH-nah): frog
las rosas (lahs ROH-sahs): roses
salta (SAHL-tah): jumps
señor (seh-NYOR): mister, sir
sí (see): yes
el sol (el sole): sun
todo (TOH-doh): all, everything
tremendo (treh-MEN-doh): great, tremendous
la vaca (la BAH-cah): cow